Dear Parent:
Your child's love of reading starts here!

Every child learns to read in a different way and at his or her own speed. Some go back and forth between reading levels and read favorite books again and again. Others read through each level in order. You can help your young reader improve and become more confident by encouraging his or her own interests and abilities. From books your child reads with you to the first books he or she reads alone, there are I Can Read Books for every stage of reading:

SHARED READING
Basic language, word repetition, and whimsical illustrations, ideal for sharing with your emergent reader

BEGINNING READING
Short sentences, familiar words, and simple concepts . for children eager to read on their own

READING WITH HELP
Engaging stories, longer sentences, and language play for developing readers

READING ALONE
Complex plots, challenging vocabulary, and high-interest topics for the independent reader

ADVANCED READING
Short paragraphs, chapters, and exciting themes for the perfect bridge to chapter books

I Can Read Books have introduced children to the joy of reading since 1957. Featuring award-winning authors and illustrators and a fabulous cast of beloved characters, I Can Read Books set the standard for beginning readers.

A lifetime of discovery begins with the magical words "I Can Read!"

Visit www.icanread.com for information
on enriching your child's reading experience.

CH

Amelia Bedelia
Goes Camping

by Peggy Parish
pictures by Lynn Sweat

HarperCollins*Publishers*

Watercolor paints and a black pen were used for the full-color art.

HarperCollins®, 🐿️®, and I Can Read Book® are trademarks of HarperCollins Publishers Inc.

Library of Congress Cataloging-in-Publication Data
Parish, Peggy.
    Amelia Bedelia goes camping / by Peggy Parish ; pictures by Lynn Sweat.
        p.   cm. — (An I can read book)
    "Greenwillow Books."
    Summary: As always, Amelia Bedelia follows exactly the instructions given to her on a camping trip, including pitching a tent and rowing boats.
        ISBN-10: 0-688-04057-8 (trade bdg.) — ISBN-13: 978-0-688-04057-4 (trade bdg.)
        ISBN-10: 0-688-04058-6 (lib. bdg.) — ISBN-13: 978-0-688-04058-1 (lib. bdg.)
        ISBN-10: 0-06-051106-0 (pbk.) — ISBN-13: 978-0-06-051106-7 (pbk.)
        [1. Amelia Bedelia (Fictitious character)—Juvenile fiction. 2. Camping—Juvenile fiction. 3. Camping—Fiction. 4. Humorous stories.] I. Sweat, Lynn, ill. II. Title.
PZ7.P219 Ao 1985   84-007979
[E]—19   CIP
                                                                                                                                  AC

❖

Originally published by Greenwillow Books,

an imprint of HarperCollins Publishers, in 1985.

12 13 LP/WOR 30 29 28 27

For Rebecca and Alex Gushin
with love
—P.P.

To James Barker
—L.S.

"Hurry up, Amelia Bedelia,"
called Mr. Rogers.

"I'm coming, I'm coming,"
said Amelia Bedelia.

"Did we get everything?"
asked Mrs. Rogers.

"I would say so,"
said Amelia Bedelia.

"Good," said Mr. Rogers.

"It's time to hit the road."

"Hit the road?"

asked Amelia Bedelia.

"All right." She picked up a stick.

And Amelia Bedelia hit the road.

"Stop that!" shouted Mr. Rogers.

"Get into the car."

Amelia Bedelia got into the car.

"I'm so excited," she said.

"I've never been camping."

"You will have fun," said Mrs. Rogers.

They rode for a long time.

Finally Mr. Rogers stopped the car.

"Wake up, Amelia Bedelia,"

said Mrs. Rogers. "This is it."

Amelia Bedelia looked all around.

"But where is the camp?"

she asked.

"The camp is in the car,"

said Mr. Rogers.

"In the car!" said Amelia Bedelia.

"We're going to camp in the car?"

"The things we need to make the camp are in the car," said Mr. Rogers.

"Make the camp!"

said Amelia Bedelia.

"We have to make the camp?"

"Just forget it," said Mr. Rogers.

"I'll put the tent here.

We can pitch it later."

"All right," said Amelia Bedelia.

"Now let's have some fun,"

said Mr. Rogers.

"Let's catch some fish."

"I've never caught fish,"

said Amelia Bedelia.

"Is it like catching a ball?"

Mr. Rogers laughed.

"It's more fun," he said.

"I will show you how."

"Did you bring any cookies?"

asked Mrs. Rogers.

"Yes," said Amelia Bedelia.

"I made up a new kind."

Amelia Bedelia got the cookies.

"Chocolate!" said Mr. Rogers.

"My favorite."

He took a bite.

"They are so crunchy!" he said.

"That's the potato chips,"

said Amelia Bedelia.

"I do love potato chips.

I put in a whole bag.

I call them chocolate chip cookies."

Mr. and Mrs. Rogers

looked at each other.

"Call them what you like,"

said Mrs. Rogers.

"Just make them often."

"Bring them along

and follow me," said Mr. Rogers.

"Let's find a good fishing spot."

They walked along the bank.

After a bit, Mr. Rogers stopped.

He looked at the water.

"This looks good," he said.

Amelia Bedelia stopped.

"I see one! I see a fish,"

she said. "I'll catch it."

"Wait!" said Mr. Rogers.

But Mr. Rogers was too late.

Amelia Bedelia was in the water.

"Here, fishy. Here, fishy," she called.

Then she grabbed the fish.

"I caught it!" she yelled.

"What a big one!" said Mrs. Rogers.

Amelia Bedelia looked at the fish.

The fish looked at Amelia Bedelia.

"All right," said Amelia Bedelia.

"Away you go."

The fish swam away.

"Amelia Bedelia!" yelled Mr. Rogers.

"Why did you do that?"

Amelia Bedelia looked surprised.

"Why not?" she said.

"You just said to catch a fish.

I did that."

"Oh, go away," said Mr. Rogers.

"Thank you," said Amelia Bedelia.

"I am wet. I do need to change."

Amelia Bedelia started to leave.

"Oh, Amelia Bedelia,"

said Mrs. Rogers.

"Please start a fire in the grill."

"Use pine cones to start it,"

said Mr. Rogers.

"And put on some coffee."

"All right," said Amelia Bedelia.

Amelia Bedelia walked to the car.

She changed into dry clothes.

"Now," said Amelia Bedelia,

"I'll surprise Mr. Rogers.

I'll pitch that tent."

She walked over to the tent.

"Shoot," said Amelia Bedelia.

"I can't even lift it."

"Need some help?" said someone.

Amelia Bedelia turned around.

"Who are you?" she asked.

"I'm Harry," said one boy.

"I'm Mike," said the other boy.

"I'm Amelia Bedelia,"

said Amelia Bedelia.

"Amelia Bedelia!" said Harry.

"We've heard about you."

"You have?" said Amelia Bedelia.

"That's nice.

Now will you help me

pitch this tent?"

"Where do you want to pitch it?"

asked Mike.

"The big thing is to pitch it,"

said Amelia Bedelia.

"It can come down

where it wants to."

The boys grinned at each other.

"Okay, let's do it," said Harry.

They caught hold of the tent.

They all picked it up.

And they pitched that tent.

"Hooray!" said Amelia Bedelia.

"We did it!"

"Maybe we should pitch it again,"

said Mike.

"Why?" said Amelia Bedelia.

"It's in the bushes," said Harry.

"That's a good place for it,"
said Amelia Bedelia.

"It's out of the way."

31

"Hey," said Mike.

"Mom is calling us."

"Thank you for helping me,"
said Amelia Bedelia.

She watched the boys go.

"I had better get that fire started,"

said Amelia Bedelia.

She got some wood

and pine cones.

She put them in the grill.

"Live and learn,"

said Amelia Bedelia.

"I didn't know pine cones

could start a fire.

I want to see this."

Amelia Bedelia sat down.

She waited and waited.

But the fire did not start.

Suddenly she jumped up.

"The coffee!" she said.

"I forgot to put on the coffee."

She poured the coffee

on the pine cones.

"Now it should start," she said.

Mr. and Mrs. Rogers walked up.
"Why isn't the fire burning?"
asked Mrs. Rogers.
"The pine cones haven't started
it yet," said Amelia Bedelia.
"Did you try using a match?"
asked Mr. Rogers.

"You didn't tell me to do that,"
said Amelia Bedelia.
"Never mind, I'll do it,"
said Mr. Rogers.
"You put on some coffee."
"I did," said Amelia Bedelia.
"Didn't I put on enough?"

"Oh, go jump in the lake,"

said Mr. Rogers.

Amelia Bedelia stamped her foot.

"I will not," she said.

"I have no more dry clothes."

Mr. Rogers laughed.

"You win," he said.

"Can you row a boat?"

"Certainly," said Amelia Bedelia.

"Use any of the boats,"

said Mr. Rogers. "Have fun."

Amelia Bedelia found the boats.

"I'll just use all of them,"

she said.

She pushed the boats

this way and that.

The boats were rowed.

Amelia Bedelia went back

to Mr. and Mrs. Rogers.

"That was fun," she said.

"What is next?"

"I need the tent stakes,"

said Mr. Rogers.

"I'll get them," said Amelia Bedelia.

She ran to the car.

She brought back a package.

"Here," said Amelia Bedelia.

Mr. Rogers opened the package.

"What in tarnation!" he said.

"Didn't I cut them right?"

asked Amelia Bedelia.

"They look like tents to me."

"How am I going to pitch the tent?"
asked Mr. Rogers.

"Don't fret," said Amelia Bedelia.

"I pitched the tent."

Mr. Rogers looked.

"Where is the tent?" he asked.

"In the bushes,"

said Amelia Bedelia.

"Just where it landed."

"That does it!"

shouted Mr. Rogers.

He stamped off.

Mrs. Rogers went after him.

"Why is he so upset?"

asked Amelia Bedelia.

"I was just trying to help him."

Mr. and Mrs. Rogers came back.

"It's all right, Amelia Bedelia,"

said Mrs. Rogers.

"We can sleep under the stars."

"I'll help you get

the sleeping bags,"

said Mr. Rogers.

"I can do it," said Amelia Bedelia.

She went to the car.

Amelia Bedelia came back slowly.

She was carrying some bags.

"Shhh," she whispered.

"I think they are sleeping.

But how can you tell?"

Mr. and Mrs. Rogers stared
at Amelia Bedelia.
Then Mrs. Rogers said,
"Never mind, Amelia Bedelia."
"I'll get this camp shipshape,"
said Mr. Rogers.
"That sounds like fun,"
said Amelia Bedelia.
"What kind of ship shape
will we make?"
"You have done enough,"
said Mr. Rogers.
"I'll do this."

Amelia Bedelia walked away.

"I don't know much about camping,"
she said. "But I do know one thing.
It's time to eat."

Amelia Bedelia bustled around.

She did this and that.

Finally she had everything ready.

"Mr. and Mrs. Rogers,"
called Amelia Bedelia.
"It's time to eat."
"I'm sure ready,"
said Mrs. Rogers.
She and Mr. Rogers came.

"Fried chicken! Stuffed eggs!"
said Mr. Rogers. "What a feast!"
All three ate and ate.
"Now I'm stuffed," said Mr. Rogers.

"There's one more thing,"
said Amelia Bedelia.
"I'll go and get it."

Soon she came back singing,

"Happy birthday to you!"

"My birthday!" said Mr. Rogers.

"I forgot my birthday."

"Blow out the candles,"

said Mrs. Rogers.

"And cut the cake."

Mr. Rogers did just that.

Then he said, "Amelia Bedelia,

this is the best camping trip ever."

Amelia Bedelia smiled.

"Let's do it again," she said.

"I do love camping."

Read all the books about
Amelia Bedelia

Amelia Bedelia
by Peggy Parish
pictures by Fritz Siebel

Thank You, Amelia Bedelia
by Peggy Parish
pictures by Barbara Siebel Thomas

Amelia Bedelia and the Surprise Shower
by Peggy Parish
pictures by Barbara Siebel Thomas

Come Back, Amelia Bedelia
by Peggy Parish
pictures by Wallace Tripp

Play Ball, Amelia Bedelia
by Peggy Parish
pictures by Wallace Tripp

Teach Us, Amelia Bedelia
by Peggy Parish
pictures by Lynn Sweat

Good Work, Amelia Bedelia
by Peggy Parish
pictures by Lynn Sweat

Amelia Bedelia Helps Out
by Peggy Parish
pictures by Lynn Sweat

Amelia Bedelia and the Baby
by Peggy Parish
pictures by Lynn Sweat

Amelia Bedelia Goes Camping
by Peggy Parish
pictures by Lynn Sweat

Merry Christmas, Amelia Bedelia
by Peggy Parish
pictures by Lynn Sweat

Amelia Bedelia's Family Album
by Peggy Parish
pictures by Lynn Sweat

Good Driving, Amelia Bedelia
by Herman Parish
pictures by Lynn Sweat

Bravo, Amelia Bedelia!
by Herman Parish
pictures by Lynn Sweat

Amelia Bedelia 4 Mayor
by Herman Parish
pictures by Lynn Sweat

Calling Doctor Amelia Bedelia
by Herman Parish
pictures by Lynn Sweat

Amelia Bedelia, Bookworm
by Herman Parish
pictures by Lynn Sweat

Happy Haunting, Amelia Bedelia
by Herman Parish
pictures by Lynn Sweat

Amelia Bedelia, Rocket Scientist?
by Herman Parish
pictures by Lynn Sweat

Amelia Bedelia Under Construction
by Herman Parish
pictures by Lynn Sweat

Peggy Parish

was the author of many books enjoyed by children of all ages. Among her easy-to-read books are a number of beloved books about Amelia Bedelia. Originally from Manning, South Carolina, Peggy Parish taught school in Texas, Oklahoma, Kentucky, and New York.

Lynn Sweat

has illustrated many Amelia Bedelia books, including *Bravo, Amelia Bedelia!*; *Good Driving, Amelia Bedelia*; *Amelia Bedelia's Family Album*; and *Amelia Bedelia and the Baby*. He is a painter as well as an illustrator, and his paintings hang in galleries across the country. He and his wife live in Connecticut.